TiDY

Emily Gravett

Simon & Schuster Books for Young Readers

NEW YORK LONDON TORONTO SYDNEY NEW DELHI

Deep in the forest lived a badger named Pete,
who tidied and cleaned and kept everything neat.

He tidied the flowers by checking each patch,
and snipping off any that didn't quite match.

He tidied the fox by grooming his fur,
he untangled each knot
and each twig and each burr.

He tidied the birds,
from the big to the small,
by brushing their beaks
and then bathing them all.

He picked up stray sticks,
he swept and he rubbed.

He polished the rocks,
and he scoured and he scrubbed.

So when a leaf fell,

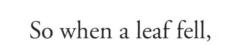
well . . .

But still he wasn't happy,
now the trees looked bare and scrappy.
And so, to make it all look neat,
Pete undertook a MIGHTY feat. . . .

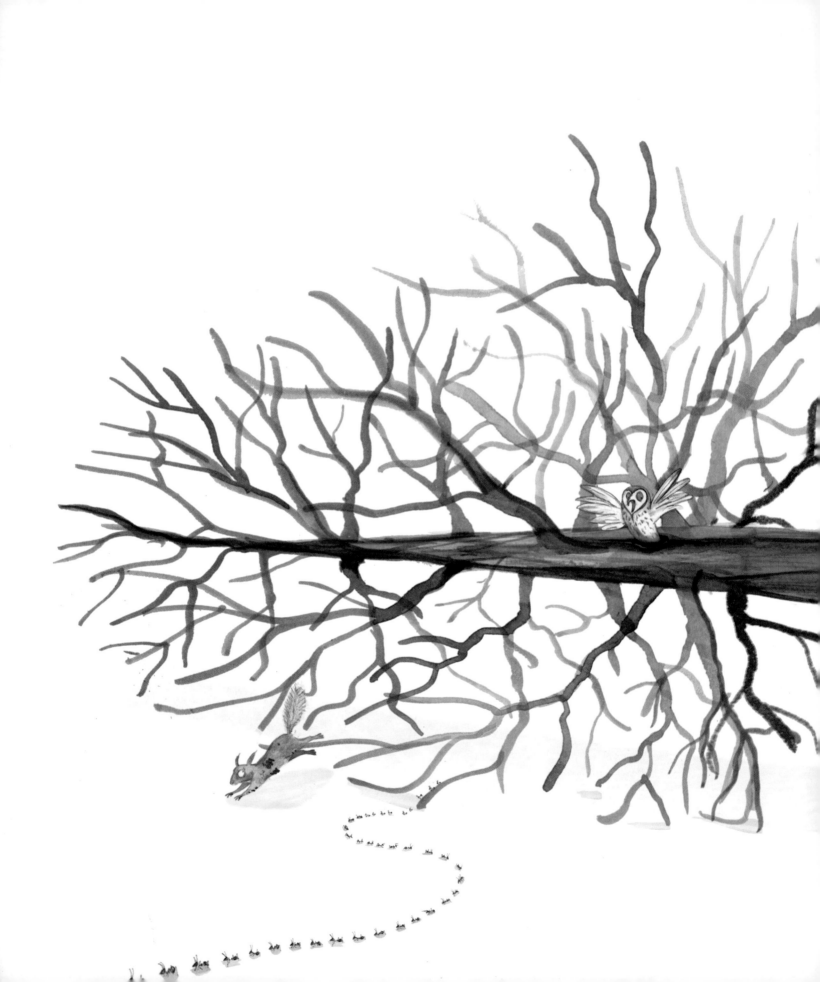

He dug up
        every
             single
                  tree!

But then it rained.

There was a

FLOOD!

And afterward a LOT of

MUD!

Pete called in the diggers,
   he called in the mixers,

he called in the concrete,
   the rakers, the fixers.

TIDY

No mud

no leaves

no mess

no trees.

Perfectly tidy and perfectly neat.
"This forest is practically perfect," said Pete.

I'm hungry! he thought. *I deserve a treat.*
So he hunted around for something to eat.

But the beetles and worms that he usually found
were under the concrete, deep in the ground.

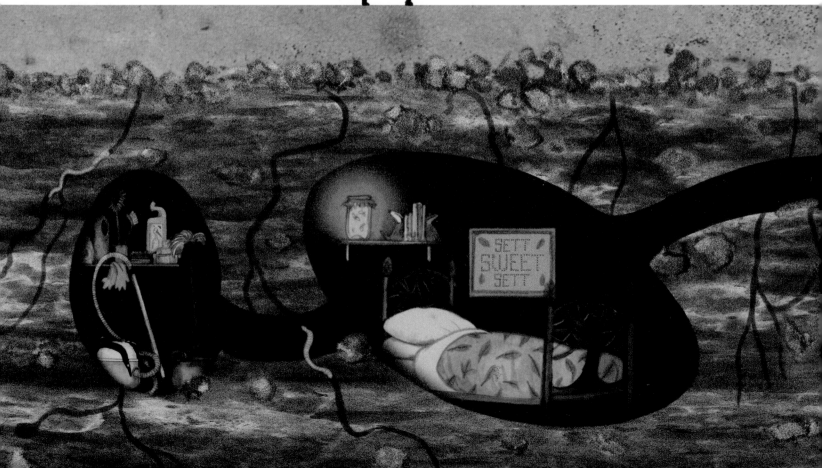

And so Pete decided to go home instead;
if he couldn't have dinner, he'd go straight to bed.

But when he arrived and took out his key,
there wasn't a door where the door used to be!

Later that night, Pete tossed and he turned.
His belly was empty, it rumbled and churned.

As he lay in his mixer, wide, wide awake
he started to think, "I have made a mistake!"

So . . .

The very next morning, when it got light,
he set about trying to put everything right.

Then the animals came—from the strong to the weak,
and they lent him a paw, or a claw, or a beak.

They put everything back, as it always had been.
(But maybe less ordered—and not quite as clean.)

And Pete? Well, he promised to tidy up less.
But if he succeeded is anyone's guess!

Keep Your
Forest
Tidy!

For Pat and Grace

SIMON & SCHUSTER BOOKS FOR YOUNG READERS
An imprint of Simon & Schuster Children's Publishing Division
1230 Avenue of the Americas, New York, New York 10020
Copyright © 2016 by Emily Gravett
Published by arrangement with Macmillan Publishers Limited
Originally published in 2016 in Great Britain by Macmillan Children's Books
First US edition 2017

SIMON & SCHUSTER BOOKS FOR YOUNG READERS is a trademark of Simon & Schuster, Inc.
For information about special discounts for bulk purchases, please contact Simon & Schuster
Special Sales at 1-866-506-1949 or business@simonandschuster.com.
The Simon & Schuster Speakers Bureau can bring authors to your live event. For more information or to book an event,
contact the Simon & Schuster Speakers Bureau at 1-866-248-3049 or visit our website at www.simonspeakers.com.
The text for this book was set in Garamond.
The illustrations for this book were rendered in pencil, watercolor, and wax crayons.
Manufactured in China
1118 MCM
4 6 8 10 9 7 5 3
ISBN 978-1-4814-8019-2 (hardcover) • ISBN 978-1-4814-8020-8 (eBook)
CIP data for this book is available from the Library of Congress.

Keep Your
Forest
Tidy!